Vanities of the Cosmos:
A Muthian Saga
By: Nathan Ritchey

Forward:

So I did not expect to write this short book. Let me first tell you, I am not a professional writer and all of this work has been done by myself, except the editing which was done by my beautiful and patient wife, Michelle.

One day in mid-September of 2024, I was sleeping and the images of the book's characters started to form into my dreams. I woke up, invigorated, and ran to my computer to start typing. The first thing I typed was horrid and barely readable. The second draft gave me new angles and characters. By the fifth draft, I had a working title, characters, and most importantly, and ending... sort of. Now, this is the tenth draft, a new name, inside joke at that, and formatting done finds me ready to write the sequel. I hope you enjoy the fast paced story, its characters, and the amount of energy it took this old man to type it all up ten times in a row.

This is dedicated to my wife, Michelle DeHart, to all the haters who said I wouldn't do anything with my life, and all those geeks in the world who have nothing but imagination and creativity to get them through this world. I love each and every one of you!

# Chapter 1: Shadows of Muth

The three moons of Muth hung low in the sky, casting an eerie, pink hued glow over the sprawling metropolis. Skyscrapers, towering like silent sentinels, stretched endlessly across the horizon, their glass facades reflecting the ghostly pink light. The air buzzed with the hum of advanced technology, a testament to the planets' unparalleled progress.

In the heart of Upper Muth, the Castle of the Empire stood as a beacon of power and authority. It was made of blood red bricks and mortar with red Wyrms etched into its outer walls and turrets. King Slinko, with his long coal-black hair, including his beard, and ghostly white pearlescent eyes, gazed out from his moka wood balcony; contemplating the fragile peace that held his world together. He wore a heavy thick red robe and on his head sat a titanium and steel crown encrusted with large black opals. Below, the city of Parl thrived, its spacecraft shipyard a hive of activity as engineers and mechanics prepared for the inevitable conflict.

The Dregogians were coming, Azmodians' prophecy has told the Muthians this. But the Muthians had no idea what to prepare for so they expected the worst they could imagine. In the city of Parl, the Duke of Parl and the Heralds of Azmodian, a police-like militia, maintained order from gangs. For example, the Top Hats who wore tall black top hats, black blazers, and talked only with sign language. Unruly citizens, who were really only panicked about the coming conflict, were also on the militias' orders.

The Duke of Parl wears a blue suit with lighter blue luminous stripes and a black tie. He was smooth, cunning, and loved to be right. The Duke lives in the Castle Rom, a large pink papered thing with a sturdy metal gate and it was adjacent to the shipyard where he kept his private craft.

The living god Azmodian also lived in Parl. His long coal-black braids, ghostly white pearlescent eyes and milky white skin played as contrast to his soft glittery pink cloak and the white pearl embedded in his forehead encrusted with gold plating. Azmodians' enclave where he lives and preaches is also where the Heralds of Azmodian live. The enclave is obtuse in shape and has three floors of solid titanium. The lighting throughout is a neon green. Azmodians' presence is a constant source of both fear and reverence among the Muthians.

As the moons reached their zenith, a sense of foreboding and dread settled over Muth. The delicate balance of power was about to be shattered, and the fate of the planet hung in the balance. In the shadows of the skyscrapers, a young warrior named Drex Loreskan prepared for the battle that would ultimately determine the future of Muth.

# Chapter 2: Invasion

Drex Loreskan stands at six feet even, milky white skin, and long black flowing hair, with ghostly pearlescent eyes to allow him to see in the dark. All Muthians have ghostly pearlescent eyes and black hair and milky white skin. Muthians, like Drex, are androgynous, and are also pansexual; which means they are attracted to others regardless of gender identity. Drex is a Herald of Azmodian, and he takes his job with the utmost seriousness. Drex, only being in his 19th cycle of Muth, is still very young and often gets chastised by his superiors. What they don't know is that Drex is the Prince of Muth, next in line to be the king.

Drex was currently at the Castle Rom in Parl, where the Duke of Parl was informing Drex and his attaché, Francine Wo who was his best friend from childhood to now, that the Dregogians had made contact with him on his vidcoms.

"They asked for our surrender or invasion," the Duke said smugly, "So I told them to Frik off and come get Friked." The Duke bellows a long laugh.

Drex was barely paying attention, as he typed on his flexpad and daydreamed about dinner at home.

"Drex, are you listening to me," the Duke said in a guff.

"I am terribly sorry, your lordship," Drex stammered as he nearly fell out of his chair. "Please continue," Drex pleaded as he remounted the chair and cleared his throat.

The Duke glared at Drex and then proceeded to speak, "As I was saying, the Dregogians are a species of creature that we have very little knowledge of. We know that they have massive ships, and

that they intend to destroy us as a race." The Duke looked pensive as he said the last part about racial eradication, and Francine passed out from the fear of the image in her head of just that.

Drex, fanning the fainted Francine, said, "I shall report this back to the Heralds and then to the King himself. The matter will be dealt with in a very quick fashion I can assure you, your lordship."

Francine Wo was considered beautiful by the Muthian standard with short cut black hair that left her bangs hiding crystal pearlescent eyes and soft milky white skin. She was also very well liked by almost all of Muth, most especially by the Duke of

Parl and Azmodian, who had called her the keystone to the future of Muth more than once, but she never understood what that meant. When she joined the Heralds, Dex was over the moons happy about it and immediately requested her as his attache.

War, Drex had never been in a war before. The thought made him both terrified and giddy. He had to get to the Heralds enclave and report to his superiors what the Duke had told him and Francine. Drex got on his speeder, a hover bike for one, and nodded to Francine.

"I'll tell the Heralds, you ride on to Upper Muth and tell the King," Francine said into her intercom to Drex. "I don't think Slinko needs to see me faint, and you have a higher chance of getting on the front lines if you are at the Castle."

"Good luck and travel safe," Drex said into his intercom and then sped away with a flash of white light from his speeders' impulse burst.

It was the 9th day of the 9th cycle of the year 20CE(Conquest Era) and Drex knew that war would begin in a few hours now. King Slinko, who was also Drexs' father, had informed the people of Muth through their flexpads and interscope sets in their homes, that war was imminent and the military was to be formed through a draft. Drex needn't wait for a draft to get his marching orders. He was on the front lines and in command of the Heralds; finally. He had the power to control the outcome of the war, or so he thought.

The Dregogians. From the moment Drex had seen them he knew they were different then the Muths. With their blonde and lime green hair, almond tan skin, and fiery red glowing eyes; they looked like the demons, not the Muthians. They were big, most of the males were six foot three or taller, and they all had solid muscle. Drex had learned that they had come from the planet called Gonk, and their planet had exploded with the supernova of their two suns. Drex did not know what a sun was, but he knew it was hot and could explode, thus making the Dregogians sound so much more dangerous.

The first ship that entered the atmosphere of the Muth planet was the size of six Banther Wyrms sewn together. The dark brown ship was impressive and Dex saw that it was using magic to create

fuel for its propulsion. Drex had never seen such a large ship before and he knew immediately that thousands of Dregog warriors were going to be on that ship.

Herald Francine ran into the main hall of the enclave and slammed her fist down on the red button to call for an emergency. "The Dregogians are here," Francine screamed into the intercom, the panic very clear in her voice.

"Francine, get the mechs ready for battle," Drex ordered, "It's time to go to war!"

# Chapter 3: Gonk

The Dregogians, with their blonde and green hair, almond tan skin, and fiery red glowing eyes were a formidable foe. Their magick and advanced spacecraft made them a constant threat to enemies. On their vibrant, luminous, and lush home planet of Gonk, the Republic of Dregog prepared for war, their blood-red armor cleaning under the light of two suns. The Republic of Dregog is a huge military complex with many steel buildings and domes flying golden banners depicting the Dregog red star.

A pack of creatures with dark blue scales, black manes, and dirty white squared teeth called Mandle Brawn gallop into the opening field to the Dregogian base. On their backs sat Sara


Polamet, Trok Polamet, and little Shy Polamet who had just turned nine years old. As they rode towards the base a tremor suddenly shook the ground and Shy's Mandle Brawn took off like grease lightning towards the shipyards.

Sara and Trok tried to usher their Mandle Brawn to follow their daughter but the creatures weren't having it. The Mandle Brawn reared back on their back hooves and thrashed wildly with their front hooves facing each other. Sara fell off backwards, landing on the hard ground with a sickening thud, her back broken instantly. Trok reached out to try to catch her before she fell and also fell from his Mandle Brawn, breaking his neck which killed him. The Mandle Brawn gallops towards the shipyard, trampling Sara to death, purple blood splashing over the entire scene including the frenzied creatures.

The three Mandle Brawn and Shy reach the shipyard at the same time. General Skar Wammgarden is working on a spacecraft landing gear when the three and Shy arrive. He stops them and pulls the very shaken young girl into his arms.

"Sh-sh-sh there there young lady," the General comforts, "What seems to be the matter here."

Shy stops sobbing long enough to say, "My Mum and Da were riding with me for my birthday and...." Skar pulled the little girl into his chest and held her. He looked at the Mandle Brawn covered in purple gore and knew that her parents were gone forever. Suddenly the disaster alarms blair and all hell breaks loose as the entire population of the Republic of Dregog runs towards the shipyards. Skar's crew heads towards the ship he is working on prepared to flee from some unknown to Skar, danger.

"General, the planet is lost. The suns are going to supernova," Loopy the Mystic to his crew screams as he gets aboard the ship.

"Holy Fuck," Skar exclaims. "Come on then little girl with the worst luck ever it's time to fucking go!"

All the crafts lift off and speed towards empty space away from Gonk. As if the suns are sentient they implode and the shockwaves vaporize the planet Gonk.

"Bye bye Mum and Da," Shy says while looking at a vidport of the explosions behind her. "I love you."

# Chapter 4: Fight in the Shipyard

Corporal Shy Polamet stood on the lip of the ship's hatch and breathed in the alien air. Without a sun, it was next to impossible to see anything at first. Slowly, her vision allowed her to make out the city before her. Low light emanated from the tall skyscrapers and holopixels that played in loops in the sky.

These Muthians were technologically advanced compared to Shy and her people and they had made long strides in the advancement of weapons she had heard. Shy reached up to scratch her Jaarl cats' chin. The cat had been a stowaway all those years ago when her planet Gonk had died along with her parents.

"You see Womak, it's just like I told you," Shy said to her Jaarl cat.

Shy had been on this ship since she was nine with Womak, who was a kitten back then like herself. Now the Jaarl cat was eight feet tall, gray, with no fur except for the fluff on her tail which was ball shaped and bright orange.

There were no nights and days on Muth, just cycles, something that was very foreign to the Dregog people. The Republic of Dregog had taken over Gonk in the olden days and then, two thousand generations later, fled the planet in search of a new home. After eleven years in space, the General had found Muth.

The initial battle was about to commence and Drex and the Heralds of Azmodian had gathered every able bodied Muthian to fight. The battle takes place in the sprawling shipyard outside the city of Parl, where the Muthians have established the fortified base of the Heralds of Azmodian. The Muthians deploy their towering mech, each equipped with advanced weaponry and shields. The mechs move in a coordinated formation, their metal feet pounding the ground.

In response, the Dregogians unleash their magick. Mystical runes glow on the ground as they summon elemental forces. Fireballs and lightning bolts light up the sky and streak across the battlefield, targeting the advancing mechs.

The Muthians use their technology to gain the upper hand. Drones swarm the battlefield, providing real-time data and targeting assistance. Laser cannons mounted on the mechs fire with pinpoint accuracy, taking out the propulsion engines of the

Dregogians space crafts. The huge crafts begin to land in the shipyard of Parl, and Dregogian warriors spill out in the hundreds. They counter the firepower of the mechs with powerful magickal spells. A group of Mystics, with their blonde and lime green mohawks, rune covered almond skin, and their fiery glowing red eyes, begin to chant in unison, creating a massive energy shield around the warriors and crafts that deflects the Muthians' continued attacks. Then the Mystics, wearing silky golden and red suits of armor, summon a heavy wind storm that topples some of the smaller mechs.

Smaller spacecraft speeds out of the massive Dregogian ships and fires plasma beams at the Muthian troops. The Muthians respond by launching anti-aircraft missiles from hidden turrets, creating a chaotic aerial dogfight.

The battlefield outside the city of Parl was a cacophony of chaos and destruction. Muthian mechs clashed with Dregogian magick, and the air was thick with the acrid smell of burning metal and ozone. Amidst the turmoil, Francine Wo fought with unwavering determination. Francine piloted her mech, which was solid gunmetal black with glowing red and green accent lights strewn across the mech's body and bright clear colored energy shield around the outside of the mech, with precision. Her eyes scan the battle for threats. She had been in countless battles, but this one felt different. The Dregogians were cruel and relentless, their magick tearing through the Muthians' ranks with devastating efficiency.

Spotting a group of Dregogian Mystics preparing a powerful spell, Francine knew she had to act or Drex and the senior members of the Heralds would die. She maneuvered her mech towards the Mystics, firing her cannons to disrupt their concentration. The ground rumbled with explosions around her, but she pressed on, determined to protect her leaders.

As she closed in on the Mystics, a massive fireball, conjured by their combined magick, struck the front of Francine's mech. The force of the explosion sent her mech crashing backwards to the ground, its armor melting in the intense heat. Francine struggled to free herself from the harness and buckles of the wreckage. With a defiant scream she emerged from the fully engulfed mech, her body battered and bloody. She raised her laser sword and sprinted at the Mystics.

General Skar Wammgarden of the Dregogians saw Francine and launched a spell of large razor sharp blades at her. Francine never had a chance, as the blades sliced off her arms, legs and head in an explosion of yellow blood and grime. Skar laughed menacingly, then turned and walked into the city of Parl. Drex screamed as he watched his closest friend get obliterated. He turned his mech towards the Mystics and with one accurate shot, left nothing of them for the Dregogians to collect.

"Fall back to Parl," Drex shouted into his mechs' intercoms. "We never expected such relentless and extreme power."


Smoke billowed from the shipyard and the wreckage of surrounding buildings. The streets were littered with debris and the remnants of the fierce battle between the Muthians and the Dregogians. The air was thick with the acrid smell of burning metal, magickal sulfurs, and the cries of the maimed and wounded.

The loss of Francine Wo was a heavy blow to the Muthian people. Her bravery and sacrifice had inspired many, but her death left a void that was hard to fill. Her comrades gathered around her corpse, paying their respects before moving on to continue fighting.

# Chapter 5: The Battle for Parl

The city of Parl, a sprawling metropolis with towering skyscrapers and once a hub of activity, was now a ghost town. The tension was thick as the Muthian mechs marched towards the city, their metallic forms glinting off the neon city lights. Above the mechs, Dregogian spacecraft hover, preparing to unleash their magickal arsenal.

"We must hold the city," the Duke of Parl says over his loudspeaker. "If the city falls, then we all are as good as ghosts."

Drex gets on a private channel on his intercoms and says to the Duke, "They killed our comrades, but not our spirits." "Take some of the laser cannon turrets to the top of those skyscrapers, and we will pin them in!"Drex told some soldiers that had arrived from the shipyards. "Mechs, on me," Drex said into his loud speaker. Three platoons of mechs

formed into a "V" shape behind Drex's mech, the sound of them walking was deafening.

Dregogian Mystics and foot soldiers dressed in head to toe blood red heavy armor began to make it into Parl, some riding Jaarl cats wearing armor; their furry balled tails now covered with mace like weapons.

The Mystics, who had been whispering a chant, shouted out,"Dragoons!" Out of the shadows, four ravenous phantom dragons roared to life.

"Holy Shit," Drex screamed, "Shields up," he frantically said into the intercoms.

The dragons breathed invisible fire at the mechs, the flames bent off the shields of the mechs

and scorched the surrounding buildings. Holoscreens above some of the shorter buildings exploded in sparks of electricity, metal, and glass.

"Concentrate all firing on those blasted dragons," Drex shouted into the intercoms. The mechs took aim and fired continued bursts of lasers at the dragons, but the lasers went through the dragons unfazed, exploding buildings and killing Muthian troops.

A Herald named Fleck, inside a mech, screamed into his intercoms, "Drex, it's no use. The weapons can't hurt them!"

Drex took a moment to think. "It must be the dragons are using the life force of those damn Mystics," Drex spoke. "Kill the Mystics and the dragons will go down!"

The mechs blasted their cannons at the Mystics, who were totally caught off guard and unprepared for such a heavy onslaught, vaporizing them to ash. The phantom dragons cried out, as though they were in pain, and then vanished back into the shadows.


Before the Muthians could celebrate their victory, the Dregogian mounted Jaarl cats pounce onto the mechs. Claws as thick as steel blades scratched at the soldiers inside the mechs.

Just then, the first signs of winter screeched into action with a blizzard tornado of icy snow. The Dregogians had never seen snow before and the Jaarl cats panicked.

General Wammgarden was on his own Jaarl cat and was doing his best to maintain control of the beast. "Retreat," he shouted in Dregogian tongue; as yet another tornado ripped through Parl towards the battlefield.


"Make for those skyscrapers," Wammgarden said in Dregog. The entire Dregogian force headed for a row of skyscrapers that sat beyond the battlefield, the same skyscrapers that the Muthians had put their turrets on.

"We have them now," exclaimed the Duke with a smirk. The turrets fired, sprays of gray bone and purple blood filled the streets as the Dregogians died.

"Blast a hole through those buildings," Wammgarden ordered. Some foot soldiers rubbed together ruins and a tidal wave of energy ripped through the skyscrapers like tissue paper.

The Dregogians fled through the rubble and headed towards the Underverse.

"Should we pursue them, Drex," Fleck inquired.

"No, this weather is only the beginning of winter, brother," Drex said back. "Everybody to the Castle Rom," Drex ordered in his loud speaker. For now this battle was at a stand still.

# Chapter 6: Of Winter and Wyrms

Winter on Muth is a harsh and unforgiving season that comes in one long, relentless cycle. The temperature plummets, and the landscape is blanketed in thick snow and ice. The sky is perpetually overcast, sending a gloomy pall over the entire land. Both the Muthians and the Dregogians must contend with the brutal cold while continuing their bitter conflict. The Muthians have fortified their position at Castle Rom with advanced technology. Heated bunkers and energy shields protect them from the worst of the cold, but resources are dwindling, and the harsh winter is taking its toll on the morale of the troops. The Dregogians rely on caves and their magick to survive the winter. They have created magickal wards, dense

green walls of lush vines and moss, to keep the cold at bay and use enchanted fires to stay warm. However, they too are running low on supplies, and the constant need to maintain their magickal defenses is draining the Mystics' energy.

A massive blizzard sweeps across the battlefield, reducing visibility to near zero. Both sides are forced to hunker down, but the Muthians see an opportunity to launch a surprise attack using their drones' heat vision capabilities to navigate through the storm.

The mechs, now frozen in place, have become useless to the Muthians. Sending a platoon of soldiers on foot, led by Drex, the Muthians sneak up on the cave system outside the Underverse.

The Dregogians' constant use of magick finally takes a toll on the Mystics and their wards against the cold falter then fall. A blast of freezing air splays into the caves, within it the platoon of laser sword welding Muthians enter, taking out the dozen or so Mystics who are exhausted and easy prey. As a frenzy of laser swords and magick spells fill the now freezing cold caverns, a call to Drex comes into his intercoms.

"Drex, there is a cache of supplies in the furthest cave system of the Underverse." The voice of Fleck echos through the cavern. All the Muthians and the Dregogians hear Drexs' intercoms and there is a moment of pause, before a desperate race ensues as Muthians and Dregogians alike scramble to secure the resources. Skirmishes break in and out, and the harsh winter conditions make every step treacherous.

The battle for the supplies reaches its peak as both sides converge on the cache. Just as a soldier from the Muthians lays his hands on the cache, the ground begins to tremble below them all. Suddenly, a horde of Banther Wyrms, their snowy blue skin, massive mouths, and multiple columns of teeth menacingly sharp, emerges from beneath the blood stained snow and ice. Screaming Muthians and

Dregogians start to retreat backwards but their escape is closed off by the Wyrms. Drex and Shy both see a small cabin about three meters away and begin sprinting towards it. Shy whistles while running and her Jaarl cat Womak runs in and she jumps on her back. She speeds by the cache of supplies, and while in motion, clips a harness onto the cache dragging it behind Womak. Shy and Womak reach the

cabin first. Shy jumps off her companion and they dart into the cabin pulling the supplies in with them. Just as Shy is about to slam the door shut, Drex explodes into the cabin slamming and locking the door behind him.

"Easy Dregogian," Drex says in a nervous tone. "We are both going to have to survive off those supplies while those damn Wyrms are out there."

Drawing a dagger out of her boot, Shy slams Drex against the door and places the cool blade against his throat. "Not if I slay your demon ass here and send out your corpse for those abominations to devour," Shy growls.

"Let's not be hasty," Drex begs, "I don't think you will survive long during the winter and I am no demon."

Shy thinks for a moment. It is true that she has no idea how long both the Wyrms and the weather would last outside. Nor

did she know what the Wyrms were capable of. Not to mention this Muthian was cute, and she could learn much about the Muthians from him.

"Very well," she sneered, "I offer a temporary truce between ourselves." Shy put the blade back in her boot sheath, and turning to Womak said, "Womak will watch you and if you make any wrong move, she will gut you like a fish." Shy patted Womak on her side panel of armor with a smile on her face.

"Sounds fair to me," Drex said in a half sigh of relief. If it had to be here with this beautiful, but clearly crazy Dregogian, or outside in the bitter cold with the Banther Wyrms, he was thankful for his choices' outcome.

# Chapter 7: Getting to Love You

The harsh winter on Muth has forced the Muthians and the Dregogians to seek shelter. Drex, Shy, and Womak have formed an unlikely truce, finding themselves trapped by Banther Wyrms and the cold in a small, secluded cabin. The wind howls outside, and snow piles up against the door. Inside, a fire made by Shy's magick crackles in the hearth, casting a warm glow over the room and making the three of them happy and friendly. Drex and Shy sit close to the fire, Womak leaning against Shy.

As Drex gazes into the fire, "It's hard to believe that just a few cycles ago, we were trying to kill each other."

Shy smiles softly, "War does that to people. It makes enemies out of those who might have been friends in another life."

Drex turned slightly to look at Shy and said, "I never thought I would say this, but I am glad we found each other. You've shown me that not all Dregogians are monsters sent to destroy us like I was told to believe."

Shy reached out and touched Drex's hand, "And you've shown me that Muthians are not the demons we have been led to believe. You're brave, compassionate, and...kind."

Drex feels warmth spreading through him at her touch. He takes her hand in his, their fingers intertwining.

"We've both lost so much to this war. But maybe, just maybe, we can find something worth holding onto," Drex says softly.

Shy leans in closer to Drex, "I think we already have. Being with you, Drex, it feels so...right. Like we were meant to find each other in all this chaos."

Drexs' heart races as he looks into Shy's glowing red eyes, seeing the same emotions reflected back at him. "Shy, I don't know what the future holds, but I want to face it with you," Drex says with a sigh. "Together, we can find a way to end this war and build a better world for both our races."

Shy whispers, "Together. I like the sound of that." They lean in, their lips meeting in a tender kiss. The fire crackles softly, and for a moment, the world outside fades away, leaving only the warmth of their newfound love. Womak leans into the couple and licks their faces.

# Chapter 8: The Festival of Azmodian

The city of Parl, still bearing the scars of war and the harsh winter, is slowly coming back to life. The Muthians have worked tirelessly to rebuild their homes and to fortify the Dukes' Castle. Despite the lingering tension with the Dregogians, the Muthians gather to celebrate the Festival of Azmodian, a time-honored tradition to honor their living god. This festival would also be the first remembering of those lost in the previous battles.

The streets are adorned with colorful lanterns and banners. Stalls line the roads where vendors offer food, trinkets, and

blessings. In the heart of the city, a grand stage has been erected, where live music is being played and the living god Azmodian is expected to make an appearance.

Drex, the young Muthian, leader of the Heralds of Azmodian, and future King of Muth stands among the crowd in front of the stage. His eyes scan the festival and he feels a mix of excitement and apprehension because Azmodian could bring both hope and fear. Drex mutters to himself, "I can't believe I am actually going to be in the presence of Azmodian. What will he say about the war? About our future?"

As the crowd dances and enjoys the festivities, a cloaked figure in radiant purple light steps into the stage and the entire crowd and band goes silent.

Raising his hands to hush the few remaining Muthians, Azmodian lays back his glittery pink hood and speaks. "My children, I am pleased to see you all gathered here today, despite our hardships. The Festival of Azmodian is a cycle of reflection, renewal, and remembrance."

The crowd murmurs in awe and reverence. Drex, feeling a surge of courage, steps forward and calls out to Azmodian.

"Father! What hope do we have in these bleak times? The war with Dregogians has left us weary, broken, and in fear."

Azmodians' gaze pierces through Drex as he steps down from the stage to stand before the young leader.

Azmodian smiles, revealing sharp white teeth.

"Drex, brave young leader, your concerns are shared by many," Azmodian speaks gently, placing a hand on Drex's purple armors' shoulder. "The path ahead is fraught with challenges indeed, but also filled with opportunities for growth and unity."

"But how can we find unity while the Dregogians seek to destroy us," Drex asked. Several Muthians echoed his question, it was apparent the crowd had become uncertain. "How can we rebuild when our resources are so scarce?"

Azmodian chuckled, " My children it is not as bleak as you deem it. Unity begins with understanding and support of your fellow Muthians. The Dregogians have weaknesses, they cannot see in the dark as we do, they are not accustomed to our planet's weather cycles and creatures. Even now there are labs full of our top techno-scientists creating new weapons. As for our resources, be wise and innovative, using what we have to rebuild stronger than ever before!"

The crowd cheered and Drex nodded with a smile on his face, feeling a sense of hope and renewed determination.

"I will do my best to lead onward," Drex said. " For our people and our planet."

Azmodian began to walk back towards the stage while saying, "Remember, Drex, the strength of the Muthian people lies not just in our technology or our might, but also in our fighting spirit and our unity. Together, we can overcome any obstacle."

The crowd erupts in cheers and clapping, as does Drex, his faith restored; for now at least. Drex stands tall, inspired by the words of his living god. The Festival of Azmodian continues, a beacon of hope and a stalwart of courage for the Muthians.

# Chapter 9: Escape

The Darkskeens, created to be super soldiers by the Muthians, have been held captive in a high-tech lab by techno-scientists and Muthian guards. The lab is a sterile and cold environment, filled with advanced technology and security measures. The Darkskeens, led by Goth Warland, have been searching and learning for a way to escape.

Goth Warland, a towering muscular figure with a commanding presence, has a blond mohawk and milky white skin with fiery red pearlescent eyes A mix of both Muthian and Dregogian DNA in his bloodstream. He wakes, realizing the guards to his cell have been

subdued. Without a word another Darkskeen enters his cell, a female, and motions him to come with her into the outer hallway. Once in the hallway, Goth sees all of the Darkskeen are free of their confinement and immediately takes charge, leading the group through the labyrinth-like corridors of the lab. Alarms blare, and red lights strobe as they make their way to the exit.

Urgently Goth whispers to the group, "Move quickly! We don't have much time before they send reinforcements."

The female says nervously, "What if we don't make it, Goth?"

Firmly Goth says, "We will make it. Trust in your training and in each other. We are stronger together."

The Darkskeens push forward, using their brute strength and enhanced magick abilities to disable security systems and take

down guards. They finally reach a massive steel door that stands between them and freedom.

"Stand back," Goth says to the group, "I'll handle this." Goth grabs a firm grip of both handles of the steel door and, using his immense strength, begins to pry open the doors; the metal groaning under the pressure. With a yowl of determination, and a final heave, the doors rip off their hinges and the Darkskeen spill out into the open air for their first time.

As they emerge from the lab, they find themselves in the midst of a battle between Muthian security and a group of Dregogian warriors, led by Corporal Shy Polamet. Shy is mounted on her Jaarl cat Womak, who is in head to tail red armor. To the Darkskeens, the Dregogians, with their magickal abilities, almond tan skin, blonde and green hair, and fiery red eyes glowing in the darkness, are a formidable sight.

Killing the last of the guards, Shy turns to Goth raising her hand, "Halt," she shouts as a blue flame sparks in her open palm. "Identify yourselves now!"

Goth speaks, "We are the Darkskeens, we seek freedom from our creators. We mean you no harm."

Skeptical, Shy asks, "Freedom? Freedom from whom?"

"From those that made us," Goth replies. "We were created to be weapons, but we choose our own path now."

Shy studies Goth for a moment, seeing both Muthian and Dregogian

traits but sensing sincerity in his words. The blue flame lowers as she says, "And what do you intend to do now?"

"We seek to control the technology of this planet so that we might find a new home for our people," Goth said with a hint of despair in his deep voice.

Shy nodded, "Very well. But know this, Darkskeen, we will not tolerate any threat to our people. Prove your intentions, and we may become allies."


Goth extends his hand in a peaceful gesture."Agreed. Let's work together to achieve our goals."

The blue flame extinguishes completely, and with a slight hesitation for a moment, Shy shakes Goths' hand, sealing the tenuous and uneasy alliance. "Corporal Shy Polamet. Pleased to meet you!"

# Chapter 10: Friend or Foe?

The city of Parl was a cacophony of chaos as the Darkskeens and Dregogians launched their assault on the Castle Rom. The night sky, illuminated a ghastly pink by the three moons of Muth, was filled with the sounds of clashing weapons and cries of battle. The towering skyscrapers and vidscreens stood as silent witnesses to the unfolding carnage.

Goth Warland, leader of the Darkskeens, stands alongside Corporal Shy Polamet of the Dregogians. They survey the battlefield, their armies ready for the impending clash.

"Darkskeens, today we fight not just for our freedom, but for a future where we can live without fear beyond Muth," Goth said to his troops. "Stand strong and show the Muthians our true spirit!"

"Dregogians, our magick and technology have brought us this far," Corporal Shy Polamet said to her soldiers. "Together with the Darkskeens, we will push back the Muthians and claim Parl for ourselves."

The combined forces of the Darkskeens and the Dregogians charge forward, their battle cries echoing through the streets. The Muthians, equipped with their advanced mechs and weaponry, meet them head-on.

Drex, wearing his purple armor, led the Muthians. His coal-black hair matted with sweat and grime

His ghostly white eyes scanned the battlefield, taking in the sight of the Darkskeens with their fiery red eyes and black jumpsuits, glowing with luminescent red panther print. Beside them, the Dregogians, with their blonde and lime green hair and blood-red armor, moved with deadly precision, their magick crackling in the air.

The Muthians fought valiantly, their advanced weaponry lit up the sky in bursts of greens, blues, and reds as they tried to hold their ground. But the combined forces of the Darkskeens and the Dregogians were relentless. Drex watched as a

group of Darkskeens, their almond tan skin glistening with purple and yellow blood under the moonlight, broke through the Muthians' lines of defense, their red eyes burning with determination.

"Hold the line!" the Duke called out in an attempt to rally the troops. But even as he spoke, a Dregogian warrior, his eyes glowing with magickal energy, unleashed a devastating spell that sent a shockwave through the Muthian ranks. The Duke barely had time to react before he was thrown to the ground, the breath knocked out of him.

As he struggled to his feet, he saw the Dregogian leader, a tall figure with lime green hair shaved up allowing for the upper portion to fall onto bare almond skin with runes and gold armor with red plating, and a commanding presence, advancing towards him. The leader's eyes blazed from inside his skull with a fierce intensity, and the Duke knew this battle would determine his fate.

With a roar, the Duke charged forward, his laser sword raised high. The clash of laser and magick echoed through the streets of Parl as the two combatants met

in a mighty duel. The air crackled with tension and lightning as the two circled each other, their eyes locked in a deadly stare.

"You've brought ruin to our land, Skar," the Duke spat, his voice filled with fury. "This ends now."

Skar Wammgarden's lips curled in a sinister smile. "Your resistance is futile, Duke. Muth will fall, and the Dregogians will reign supreme."

With a roar, the Duke lunged forward, his laser sword slicing through the air at a downward angle. Skar parried the blow with ease, his magic-infused blade shimmering with dark black energy. The two clashed again and again, each strike sending sparks flying.

"You underestimate the strength of the Muth," the Duke growled, pushing Skar back with a powerful swing. "We will never bow to your tyranny."

Skar laughed, a cold, mirthless sound. "Your defiance is

admirable, but ultimately pointless." "You will die! You will all die!" He raised his hand, and a bolt of white hot magick shot towards the Duke, who barely managed to dodge it.

The battle raged on, each man gave no quarter. Yellow and purple blood stained the ground as they exchanged blow after blow, their movements a deadly dance of skill and anticipation. The Duke's armor was battered, his breath was becoming more and more labored, coming in ragged gasps and wheezes, but he refused to yield.

"You fight well, Duke," Skar admitted, his voice tinged with respect. "But this is the end."

With a swift, brutal uppercutting strike, Skar's blade found its mark across the Dukes' now exposed chest. A spray of yellow blood decorated the front of Skar's armor. The Duke staggered, pain searing through his entire body. He fell to his knees on the cold street, his sword slipping from his grasp.

Skar stood over him, his eyes crazed and laughing maniacally. "Any last words, your lordship?"

The Duke looked up with defiance and spat out, "Get Friked!" He lifted his middle finger painstakingly.

With a final, merciless downward thrust, Skar chopped off the Dukes' head. The battlefield fell silent and all fighting ceased as the Muthians watched their friend die, a mix of grief and rage in their hearts. Dex had been surrounded by Darkskeens when the Duke went down. Seeing the man who was his boss for so many years get snuffed out he screamed.

"Nooooooo!" Drex fell to his knees and started to weep. Just then, the Heralds of Azmodian, came stomping in to reinforce the Muthians that clearly were losing. Drex saw they had lost the fight and shouted in his intercoms, "Retreat to Castle of the Empire." The battle for Castle Rom was over, but the war for Muth had only just begun.

# Chapter 11: Spy

The air was thick with tension as the Darkskeens and Dregogians marched towards the Castle of the Empire in Upper Muth. The sky above was a swirling mass of dark clouds, mirroring the chaos below. The Muthians, led by their valiant King Slinko, stood ready to defend their home.

Raising his laser sword, King Slinko, now wearing his icy blue suit of titanium armor, shouted, "For Muth! We will not let them take our land!"

The clash of metal and the roar of battle cries filled the air as the two armies collided. Amidst the chaos, Goth Warland, a formidable Darkskeen warrior, spotted King Slinko. With a determined snarl, he charged through the fray, cutting down anyone in his path.

Grabbing Slinko by the throat, Goth Warland sneered, "Your reign ends here, Slinko!"

King Slinko struggled, but Goth's

grip was unyielding. He was dragged away from the battlefield and thrown into a dark, cold cell within the Castle.

Slinko panting says, "You won't get away with this, Warland."

Goth Warland leaned in close, his eyes gleaming with malice. "Oh, but we already have..."

Slinko quickly cut him off saying, "The Dregogians have a plan, Goth. A plan that involves the termination of both the Muthians and the Darkskeens."

Goths' eyes widened in shock."Termination? But why? The Darkskeens are the Dregogians' ally!"

King Slinko smirking, "Precisely. They were created to serve us, but you have become too dangerous, your time is over. The Dregogians will rule this planet."

Warlands' mind raced. He had to find a way to warn the Muthians and the Darkskeens. The fate of Muth depended on it.

The battle raged on outside the Castle of the Empire, but deep within its stone walls, a different kind of conflict was

unfolding. Goth Warland, having captured King Slinko, now turned his attention to the Darkskeens. He knew that the Dregogians' plan for termination would soon be set into motion, and his loyalty to his own kind made him feel a sense of duty to warn his people and the Muthians.

Goth Warland made his way through the dimly lit corridors of the castle, his footsteps echoing ominously. He reached a hidden chamber where the Darkskeens had

gathered, preparing for their next move. His second in command, a slim female named Nyx, stopped talking to the group and turned, she narrowed her eyes and said, "What do we do next boss?"

Goth Warland took a deep breath, his expression serious. "Nyx, you need to listen to me. The Dregogians have a plan that involves the termination of both the Muthians and the Darkskeens."

The room fell silent as the Darkskeens processed his words. Nyx stepped forward, her gaze piercing, "Why would they do that, aren't we their allies?"

Goth sighed, "Because I know what they're capable of. They see you as a threat, and once the Muthians are defeated, they'll turn on us. We were created to serve the Muthians, but now the Dregogians fear our power."

A murmur of unease spread through the Darkskeens. Nyx's eyes flickered with a mix of anger and determination, "If what you say

is true, then we must act. We cannot allow the Dregogians to betray us."

Goth Warland nodded his head."We need to join forces with the Muthians. Together, we can stand against the Dregogians and protect our future."

Nyx considered his words, then turned to her fellow Darkskeens, "Prepare for battle. We fight not just for ourselves, but for the future of Muth. And we will not be betrayed." She turned back to Goth and said, "And you will lead us in battle!"

The Darkskeens moved with renewed purpose, their resolve strengthened by the knowledge of the impending betrayal. As they prepared to face the Dregogians, they knew that the fate of their world hung in the balance.

Meanwhile, Drex had stumbled into the secret prison, bewildered to find King Slinko locked in a cell, "Dad, what the blazes are you doing in there?"

Slinko chuckled, "I had a vacation with a friend."

"What in the hell are you talking about," Drex fumed as he found the key, a block looking thing, and opened the cell to release Slinko.

"I'll tell you everything on the quest to the armory, my boy," King Slinko mused as he walked quickly towards a hidden staircase.

# Chapter 12: Fleck Picks Wrong

The battlefield was a chaotic expanse of clashing swords and roaring warriors. The Muthians and Dregogians were locked in a fierce struggle, each side determined to claim victory.

Amidst the turmoil, the Herald Drex stood tall, his voice booming as he rallied the Muthian forces,"Hold the line! Do not let the Dregogians break through!"

His words were cut short by a

sudden, eerie silence that fell over the battlefield. The Dregogians paused, their eyes scanning the horizon for the source of the disturbance. From the shadows, the Darkskeens emerged, their dark forms blending seamlessly with the surrounding landscape.

Warland whispered, "Now. Strike swiftly and without mercy."

The Darkskeens moved with lethal precision, their ambush catching

the Dregogians off guard. Using their advanced magick they made new forms of handheld weapons, and silently with fervor assassinated two platoons of Dregogians in minutes.

Skars' eyes widened in shock as he saw his comrades fall one by one, their cries of pain echoing through the air, "To arms! Defend yourselves!"

But it was too late. The Darkskeens descended upon the Dregogians like a storm, their blades cutting through armor and flesh with terrifying ease.

General Skar Wammgarden fought valiantly, his sword clashing against the dark flaming steel of his enemies. He managed to fend off several attackers, but the sheer number of Darkskeens overwhelmed him.

A Darkskeen warrior, his eyes glowing with a fierce determination, lunged at Skar. The General parried the attack, but the force of the blow sent him staggering backward. Before he could recover, another

Darkskeen struck from the side, his blade slicing through Skar's armor and into his side with brute strength alone. General Skar Wammgarden said in shock, "No... this cannot be..."

Purple blood poured from the wound, staining the ground beneath him. Skar fell to his knees, his vision blurring as life drained from his body. The Darkskeen who had struck the fatal blow stood over him, his expression cold and unyielding. Before Skar could say anything

else Goth Warland ran his blade through the Generals' back and his heart emerged out of his chest with a gush of purple gory blood.

As Wammgarden breathed his last gasp, his body crumpled to the ground, the Darkskeens continued their assault, their ambush turning the tide of the battle. The Dregogians, now leaderless and demoralized, began to falter, their lines breaking under the relentless onslaught.

Just as it seemed the war might end here and now, a mech driven by the Herald Fleck Qunn and the entire Jaarl cat force came crashing into the battlefield.

"You fucking traitor, Fleck," said an enraged Drex in the intercoms. "I am personally going to rip your spine out!"

Shy and Womak had come into the Castle of the Empire to confront Goth Warland about working with the Dregogians, but now she saw Drex and knew she had to help him and his people defend their land, "Womak, we have to fight the Dregogians now. Can you do that," Shy sweetly talked to her Jaarl cat. Womak cooed and rubbed her head against Shys' head. "Good girl!"

Womak took two huge steps then Shy jumped on Womaks' back and the beast zipped off on foot out of the Castle of the Empires' red front gate. The first thing that they encountered was a couple foot soldiers who had lowered their weapons and defenses. Womak landed squarely on the chest of one male Dregogian, smashing him onto his back. Womak ripped his head off with a swift bite, and spit out the head. Shy slew the other two soldiers, one male and the other female, with a spell that raised gravity in a three meter cone around them by sixty percent. The purple blood oozed out of their body's and the heat intensity was rival to the smell of grossness.

The Dregogian Jaarl cat army was obliterating the Muthians and the Darkskeens and Shy was afraid that this might actually be how the light of Muth was extinguished. She had a choice to make, save Drex from Fleck and himself, or save Goth Warland and get to what was Skar's ship, but now was hers due to his brutal death.

"Darkskeens, regroup at the shipyard," Nyx shouted.

Drex looked at Goth and said, "We will cover you. Go quickly. Now!"

Drex called into his intercoms and said, "Time to show these monsters just what the spirit of Muthians can do." Give me all your fire power and grit while we cover the Darkskeens escape."

The Muthians began to launch a rocket assault on the Jaarl cats. Reprogrammed to find the cat's exact heat signatures, the rockets stopped them cold in their tracks. Jaarl cat corpses lay everywhere. There was so much

Jaarl cat blood on the Castle of the Empire walls and windows that it camouflaged the red brick an opaque purple gray color.

Drex got into his off white mech and picked up the weapon his father, King Slinko, had used to form Muth into what came before this cycle. The double bladed laser battle axe was large, heavy, and had slain over fifty red Wyrms, thirty-five Banther Wyrms, and a monster of a man named Sterns.

"You and me, Fleck," Drex challenged. "I want to teach you some loyalty!"

"Frik you, Daddy's boy," says a petulant Fleck. "Have at thee!"

Drex drove his mech at Fleck, making a chopping motion with his weapon. The battle axe bounced off the clear energy shield with a *Thung!* sound that reverberated into the cockpit of both mechs. Fleck laughed, raising his laser sword, and thrusting it forward at Drexs' face. Drex quickly moved his head to the left as the laser sword pierced through his headrest.

"Nothing you can throw at me will be good enough," Drex chortled.

"You and I were both trained by the Duke, you traitorous piece of garbage!" Drex spun his mech in a clockwise spin, extending his battle axe level with his mech waist, slicing through Fleck's energy shield and taking the left leg of the mech completely off. The mech wobbled for a moment, then slammed onto its right side with a wicked rumble that startled the remaining Jaarl cats.

Fleck unclipped his harness and fell out of his mutilated mech head first in a heap on the street.

"Please, Drex, have mercy on me," Fleck begged as he rolled onto his back looking upwards into the cold stare of Drex's eyes.

"I have no mercy to give you," Drex said somberly. "You have made your bed, now die in it!" Drex raised the right leg of his mech and stomped down on Flecks' head, a spray of brains and yellow blood stained the street and the bottom of the mech.

Shy, still mounted on Womak, sped towards Drex and said, "Get King Slinko out here. I will take him to the shipyard."

"Copy that," Drex said in his intercom. He climbed out of his less than pristine white mech and walked into the Castle of the Empire. "Dad, it's time to go," Drex shouted as he walked through the hall to the main courtyard.

"Oh my dear boy, How delightful to see you again," Slinko purred. "It's that time already?"

"Yes, sir," Drex said as he assisted the King out of the Castle.

Shy was patiently waiting just outside the Castles' doors and once King Slinko and Dex emerged, she had Womak lay down. "Okay, your Highness," Shy said as she reached out her hand to the King. "Nice and easy now."

As soon as the King was on Womak, Dex nodded at Shy. "Take care of him," Dex said with admiration in his expression. "I love you, Shy."

Shy giggled as Slinko went wide eyed. " I love you, too, Dex."

# Chapter 13: A New Threat

After getting their asses handed to them at the Castle of the Empire, the Dregogians had returned in straggles to the Underverse caves and labyrinths. Now without a leader, the Dregogians began to fight and bicker amongst themselves. A tall, muscular male Dregogian named Pith, wearing blood red armor that exposed his rippling almond tan abs. He was six feet five inches tall. He stood on a boulder, making him a giant in the cavern, and made an announcement.

"I am the Lieutenant to Wammgardens' platoon," Pith said with bravado. "So I believe I am next in line to lead our people."

The Dregogians all began to mutter and clammer about so Pith said with urgency, "All in favor say, 'aye.'" Ninety percent of the Dregogians said, "Aye."

"There it is then," Pith beamed happily. "I am the boss and I say we find reinforcements within the criminal elements here in the Underverse."

As though he had heard Pith, Maxius and the Top Hats entered the cove where the Dregogians had gathered.

"We would like to help you, our downtrodden friends," Maxius said in sign language.

"What are you getting on about with all that flapping about," Pith said sarcastically.

"It's sign language you twit," said Fern, a Muthian female, with coal-black hair in a ponytail, white pearlescent eyes, and milky white skin covered in purple and red tattoos. She wore a red mini skirt that was almost too short, a denim shirt that was buttoned to show her black lacy bra and busty cleavage, and black military boots with a dagger sheathed in the left one.

"Who the bloody hell are you?" Pith bleated.

"I am the leader of the Kerkins Organization and we are willing to assist you as much as Maxius here is too," Fern said smoothly. I will play as the voice for the Top Hats and they will be the facilitator of information and strategy, if that pleases you?"

"I speak for the Dregogians now," Pith told her, "And we agree to these terms."

Fern pursed her lips and smiled venomously. "Well if that ain't just sweetness."


Meanwhile, Shy, Goth, Nyx, and


the Darkskeens were doing maintenance and preparations to the spacecraft that they had stolen from the Dregogians, as well as the Muthian crafts. King Slingo sat in the cockpit of Shys' ship, amused with the flashing lights on the dashboard. He found the intercom button and said, "Shy, what is the plan for you and Drex?"

Shy blushed a color of pink that made her almond skin tone radiant. "I am not sure, your Highness."

"Please, call me Slinko," the King told Shy. "I suppose you intend to mate with Drex; yes?"


"I would like to just survive this war," Shy sighed. "I can't think too far into the future like that, Slinko." She stood from where she had been crouching to work, and walked over to Womak, who was eating a large piece of meat with fervent intent.

"Are we about done here," Goth interrupted, feeling awkward about the previous conversation they all had been listening to.

Shy cleared her throat in anxiety and said, "Yep, all good here."

"Good, then let's get back to Parl and the Muthians," Nyx said curtly.

They all got in the smaller of the three carrier craft that the Muthians used to travel between the different regions, and drove to the still heavily wrecked city of Parl. As they passed under the city lights, the crew readied their various weapons and runes respectively. Shy was driving the carrier, pulling into the parking station of the Heralds' enclave, she couldn't help putting a happy face on at the prospect of seeing Drex again. Drex saw the carrier parking on the vidscreen and rushed out to greet the crew and the remaining Darkskeens. Before he could say a word, Womak tackled him to the ground, licking and slobbering clear foam all over Drexs' face. Laughter filled the small parking station, reverently, for the first time since before the war had begun.

"It's nice to see you too, Womak," Drex said, his mouth half muffled by the weight of the Jaarl cats' tongue.

Shy pulled Womak off of her lover, and then helped him to his feet.

"And a hello kiss for you," Shy said, as she pressed her lips against the lips that Womak had just been licking. She spat quickly afterwards, "I guess we are that kind of couple now."

They all laughed again. It felt good to laugh, Drex thought to himself. Having Shy here with him, at the end of all this loss

and carnage, was an unforeseen bonus. Goth and Drex shook hands. Then, Nyx hugged Drex and said, "I would be amiss if I didn't think we were more family now."

Drex smiled at her, but was silenced by the King saying, "We indeed are all family now. And cheers to my son, Drex for making it all possible." Everyone except Shy gasped at the sudden revelation. "Muthians, Darkskeens, this is your future King of Muth!" Slinko was beaming from ear to ear at the news he just dropped, like a bomb, on the entire population of Muth that was present.

However, good news as it was did not last long. A row of skyscrapers suddenly exploded, sending glass in all directions.

"Contact," Drex screamed. "This is it people, the final battle is happening right now!"

A wave of Dregogians emerged from within the smoke and falling facade particles. But they did not attack, rather they formed lines like a runway along the street leading up to where Drex, Shy, Goth, Nyx, the remaining few Darkskeens, and the entire thousand and a half worn out Muthian force stood. They were ready for a hearty interaction, what they were receiving threw

them all for a loop. And then the really shocking thing happened. Riding on Jaarl cats, the Top Hats, Kerkins Organization, wearing purple and gold armor that flowed like a dress with gold boots that had purple accents down the sides, and Pith, swayed down the street towards their foes. Behind the Jaarl cats the resolute Dregogian army marched in a casual fashion.

Drex looked nervously at Shy, "What the hell is this?"

"I have no idea," Shy said, appearing to be just as stunned as Drex. "Aren't those Muthians too?"

"Yes," Drex said.

"But the worst of the worst of us," Slinko followed.

The calvary of Jaarl cats halted fifty feet from the Muthian-Darkskeen forces and Pith snarled, "Greetings scumbags. Looks like I found both leadership and friends on this goddamn planet."

Fern hopped off her Jaarl cat and danced around in a circle beside it before speaking, "You have a choice now Drex, baby. You all can leave this planet in the ships you stole from the Dregogians..."

Maxius signed, "Shame on you!" and all of the Top Hats broke into silent belly laughs.

"Or you can stay and die here and now," Fern finished, with a girlish giggle. " If it were up to me, I'd just slaughter ya all. Maxius wanted to be fair, so thus your choices. Ha, ha ha!"

Drex looked at Goth, who had been secreting a laser cannon behind his large back, then at Shy, a spell already bending the air behind the enemies backs, unbeknownst to them.

"Well, you wanna know what I think, Fern," Drex said with a

pause, and a slight nod to his dad to get down on the ground. "I think, Frik you!"

Goth shot the cannon at Pith, blowing a chunk of his face off. Pith screamed in agony, falling backwards into the puddling purple blood oozing from him. Shy had been bending a tornado of mega proportions, unleashing it now into the Dregogins, who cried out, completely surprised. Mystics and foot soldiers flew into the air in all directions, wails of horror echoed in the wake of the tornado.

"Holy friking shit," Fern exclaimed as she ducked for cover behind the Jaarl cat she had been riding. The Kerkins Organization

thugs jumped into action, shooting laser cannons and pistols at any Muthian or Darkskeen they could lay a target on. The Top Hats, looking at Maxius for guidance, stood in a huddled mass. Maxius looked at a Darkskeen coming towards him and prepared to run away. The

Darkskeen launched a lightning bolt towards Maxius, who narrowly escaped by leaping to the right. A crater replaced the ground the mute criminal had been standing on. He turned and signed, "Run away," to the dumbfounded Top Hat gang. They saw their leaders' message, and hotfooted it back towards the Underverse.

Drex and Nyx stood shoulder to shoulder taking shots at

Dregogian after Dregogian, losing complete sight of Fern, who had somehow managed to get behind the two. Fern snuck quietly like a predator animal stalking its prey.

Seconds before Fern attacked, Shy noticed her and screamed, "Drex, look out!" Drex shoved Nyx away, Ferns' dagger connecting Drexs' throat. Yellow blood splayed out from the wound while Drex gasped for air, holding onto his throat as though it would pause the flow of life draining rapidly from him. Fern laughed aloud and jumped on her Jaarl cat, The cat spread its four bat-like wings and took flight towards the Underverse.

"Drex," Shy screamed in agony and ran to her dying mate. He was dead before she ever reached him, catching his falling corpse, Shy wept at the loss. The remaining Dregogians took the pause in fighting, to return on Jaarl cats, back to the Underverse. The Muthians and Darkskeens gave chase.

"He saved me," a shocked Nyx said softly. She felt both remorse and guilt, no one had ever given their life in defense of hers and she would not forget it, or forgive Fern for what she had wrought.

Shy laid Drexs' body on the ground and pulled the dagger from the hole in his throat vowing,"I will kill Fern for this, I promise you, my love." The King wept as he circled around his son's body with Shy, Nyx, and Goth.

Gritting his teeth in rage, Goth said, "Let's finish this!"

# Chapter 14: Final Conflict

The Dregogians had barely made it back to the Underverse when Muthians started to attack. With more chaos than before, now that their recent leadership had his face blown off, the Dregogians were losing members rapidly. The Top Hats had seemingly disappeared into the labyrinth of the Underverse, ditching their supposed allies to all but perish. Goth Warland and Shy Polamet arrived in the Underverse and quickly began to hunt for Fern.

"She is going to hide well in here," Goth said to Shy. "I think we should go in teams to hunt her."

"Slinko and I will take the caverns," Shy replied. "Come on, Slinko, let's go." Slinko, now equipped with a laser battle axe, hurried to Shys' side.

"Nyx, you are with me," Goth said as he checked his laser cannons' charge.

"Copy that boss," Nyx said and pulled her a steel blade from a sheath on her back, infusing it with dark blue energy.

Blood and gore filled the maze like tunnels of the Underverse, the smell and acrid horrid tinge in Gores' nostrils. Ferns' Jaarl cat had come through this way leaving an easily trackable path.

Paw prints in sets of four at a moderate pace. Goth and Nyx were lightly jogging the tunnel following the path made by the cat, when suddenly there it stood before them.

"Fern," Goth shouted. "Time to face the reapers!" The sound of Goth's voice reverberated down the tunnel and startled the Jaarl cat, who had been facing the opposite way watching something in the distance. As the large cat turned and zeroed in on the two Darkskeen warriors, Nyx realized what the animal was watching; Fern!

"There she goes down that left hand tunnel," Nyx said with an excited tone to her voice. "I will get her, you deal with this other problem."

Goth nodded to his partner, just as the cat took off towards him.

Looking for a way to handle the situation quickly, he spotted a crystal size gemstone sticking out from the ceiling of the tunnel in the Jaarl cats path. Goth quickly shot a volley of lasers at the gemstones, loosing it free. It slammed into the cat's head, piercing its heavy armor and into its thick skull. An eye popped out and due to how close

the cat had made it to Goth, it smacked into his face with a plopping sound.

Breath rasping from the speed she had to use to catch up to Fern, Nyx was two feet from catching Fern. Fern suddenly stopped running and turned to face her purser.

"Stop, you are not going to catch me," Fern said frustrated. Fern slowly reached behind her back where she had a dagger hidden in the waistband of her mini skirt.

"I am going to make you pay for murdering Drex," Nyx screamed at Fern and took a huge breath.

"I made him a martyr," Fern giggled. "You were my target, but he had to meddle in my affairs. You should thank me."

"Thank you," Nyx said incredulously. "For what?"

Fern laughed,"For setting you free." She quickly threw the dagger at Nyx, aiming for her face. Nyx anticipated the move and dropped to one knee, letting the dagger zip over her head, clattering harmless behind her. With an elated smile of vengeance on her face, Nyx stepped the remaining distance to Fern and swung a death blow at Ferns' head, decapitating head from body.

"Good riddance," Nyx spat. "Rest in Peace Drex."

Shy and King Slinko had found the Top Hats and were quite outnumbered, which Maxius was very aware of as he signed battle instructions to the gang. Shy was thankful for Womaks' presence because she didn't know what would happen without her protector.

"Stop this," Slinko commanded the Top Hats. "I am your King, you must do my bidding." A young member of the Top Hats flipped the King off and fired a laser at Slinko. His aim was way off, the laser exploding into rocks.

Slinko swung his axe and brought down the youth in a crumpling mess.

"Slinko, get over here," Shy called to her would have been father in law. She jumped on Womaks' back and as Slinko ran towards the pair, laid Womak down so Slinko could board the cat. As soon as the King was on, the cat took off in the reverse direction that they had come like a speeder. The Top Hats attempted to give chase, but were no match for the Jaarl cats' speed. Shy breathed a sigh of relief and Slinko laughed.

Regrouping at the entrance to the Underverse, the Muthians and the Darkskeens had either killed or captured all the remaining Dregogians. Seeing that Shy and Slinko were unharmed he smiled, then laughed when he realized the war was over.

"Why are you laughing like that," Shy inquired with a pout on her face.

"Oh it's nothin," Goth Warland chortled. "Just the vanities of the cosmos!" He began to laugh again, the others laughing with him.

**The End... or is it?**

About the Author:

Nathan Ritchey lives in a three bedroom house in Southern Oregon with his wife, Michelle DeHart, and two cats, Meatball & Kasper. He is an avid Xbox player, Dungeons & Dragons fan, and die-hard Luciferian.